WONDER WOMAN

★ THE AMAZING AMAZON ★

CHEETAH UNLEASHED

WRITTEN BY
BRANDON T. SNIDER

ILLUSTRATED BY
LUCIANO VECCHIO

WONDER WOMAN CREATED BY
WILLIAM MOULTON MARSTON

STONE ARCH BOOKS
a capstone imprint

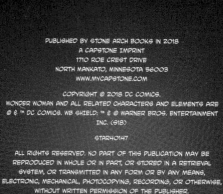

PUBLISHED BY STONE ARCH BOOKS IN 2018
A CAPSTONE IMPRINT
1710 ROE CREST DRIVE
NORTH MANKATO, MINNESOTA 56003
WWW.MYCAPSTONE.COM

STAR40147

CATALOGING-IN-PUBLICATION DATA IS AVAILABLE AT THE LIBRARY OF
CONGRESS WEBSITE.
ISBN: 978-1-4965-6529-7 (LIBRARY BINDING)
ISBN: 978-1-4965-6533-4 (PAPERBACK)
ISBN: 978-1-4965-6537-2 (EBOOK PDF)

SUMMARY: CHEETAH'S ON THE LOOSE! AFTER A DESPERATE ESCAPE
FROM PRISON, THE FELINE FELON USES A STOLEN MAP TO TRACK
DOWN PANDORA'S BOX. WHILE THE VILLAIN THINKS IT HAS THE POWER
TO MAKE HER HUMAN AGAIN, WONDER WOMAN KNOWS BETTER. CAN THE
AMAZON WARRIOR STOP CHEETAH BEFORE SHE OPENS THE LEGENDARY
ARTIFACT? OR WILL THE WORLD BE CAST INTO COMPLETE CHAOS?

EDITOR: CHRISTOPHER HARBO
DESIGNER: HILARY WACHOLZ

Printed and bound in Canada.
PA020

TABLE OF CONTENTS

With countries in chaos and the world at war, Earth faced its darkest hour. To answer its cry for help, the Amazons on the secret island of Themyscira held a trial to find their strongest and bravest champion. From that contest one warrior—Princess Diana—triumphed over all and boldly entered the world of mortals. Now her mission is to conquer villainy, defend justice, and restore peace across the globe.

She is . . .

WONDER WOMAN

★ THE AMAZING AMAZON ★

CHAPTER 1

SURPRISE ESCAPE

The halls within A.R.G.U.S. headquarters were cold and quiet as one of its top agents, Steve Trevor, made his way into the facility's sub-basement. A.R.G.U.S. was a secret government agency that watched the world for danger from its hub in Washington, D.C.

On the surface, the A.R.G.U.S. command center looked like any other run-of-the-mill office building. But there were secrets buried deep underneath. Its lower level contained a prison for super-villains.

Agent Trevor, along with a new A.R.G.U.S. recruit, was about to come face to face with one of the prison's worst criminals. As they walked down a long, brightly lit hallway, Steve sensed his companion was on edge.

"What was your name again, Officer?" Agent Trevor asked.

"Gray, sir," the new recruit answered. "Officer Patrick Gray."

"You're sweating, Patrick." Steve chuckled. "Don't worry. This'll be a piece of cake."

Officer Gray nodded nervously. "I've never seen a super-villain up close before," he said. "Especially one with claws and a tail."

Steve pointed to a pair of handcuffs in Officer Gray's hands. "Get those on her as quickly as possible and be careful. She'll try to rattle you," Steve said. "Just stay focused and this will all be over soon enough."

They arrived at the end of the hallway. A steel door opened to reveal a single prison cell. It held one of the most unpredictable criminals in the world. She rubbed her eyes and growled as the bright light blinded her. Cheetah, the feline felon, was groggy. She had just woken up from a nap.

"Patrick, meet Barbara Ann Minerva, aka Cheetah," Steve said. "Rise and shine, kitty cat. Today is your lucky day."

Cheetah moved her face close to the bars and hissed. "Leave me alone!"

"That's not going to happen. You haven't been behaving yourself lately. Scratching guards isn't something *nice* kitties do," said Steve. "We're here to help escort you to another prison. You'll be someone else's problem from now on. A.R.G.U.S. is done trying to help you change your evil ways."

HAHAHAHAHA! Cheetah cackled wildly. "*Help me?* You've tossed me in jail and thrown away the key!" she said. "Admit it, Trevor. You don't care what happens to me as long as I'm locked up." Her tail crept through the bars and tickled Steve's leg.

"Cut it out!" he exclaimed. "Or should I call my friend Wonder Woman? I bet she'd love to take you to your new home."

"Shut your mouth!" Cheetah screeched. She extended her sharp nails and showed them to Steve. "Don't *ever* say that name in front of me again, or I'll claw your eyes out."

"Take it easy, fur ball," Steve said. He nodded at Officer Gray. It was time to go.

"Cheetah, put your wrists together and slip them through the bars so I can handcuff you," said Officer Gray. His hands trembled as he gripped the electronic bracelets.

Cheetah did as she was told. "Not my kind of jewelry," she purred. "But I suppose I have no choice."

"Officer Gray, turn on the handcuffs," Steve said.

Officer Gray removed a small remote control from his pocket and pressed its buttons.

FZZZZZZZZZ! Cheetah's cuffs snapped into place. He pressed more buttons and the cuffs began to hum.

"No funny business, Cheetah. Try to escape and you'll get zapped," said Steve. "Stay calm, and this will all go smoothly."

The cell door opened and Cheetah slid out between Steve and Officer Gray. As they walked down the hallway, Cheetah eyed the remote in Gray's hand. He held it anxiously.

"First day, Officer Gray?" Cheetah whispered. Then she dropped and swept her leg across the floor, knocking Officer Gray off his feet. The remote control went flying.

Cheetah caught the remote, threw it on the ground, and crushed it with her foot. With the controls destroyed, her electronic cuffs turned off. She was finally free.

Officer Gray froze with fear. Cheetah gave him a swift head-butt, knocking him out.

"Looks like A.R.G.U.S. gave you all that fancy training for nothing," Cheetah sneered.

Steve reached into his holster to grab his Taser. "Freeze!" he shouted.

Cheetah whipped her tail into the air and knocked the weapon from his hands. While he was stunned, Cheetah kicked Steve in the stomach. He collapsed with a groan.

"What are you going to do now, little Stevie?" she mocked.

At the opposite end of the hallway, two steel doors parted to reveal three more A.R.G.U.S. officers. They were headed in Cheetah's direction, Tasers ready.

"Bring it on," she growled.

As the guards moved closer, Cheetah attacked. She jumped on one officer and flung him into his partner, knocking them both out.

Another officer tried zapping Cheetah, but she was too fast for him. She leaped across the hallway with incredible speed. Once she was close, she swiped her sharp claws across the officer's hands. He dropped his weapon and Cheetah snatched it right up.

"You want some?" she threatened.

SHZACK! Cheetah fired the weapon at the officer, sending a shock through his body.

"This won't end well, Cheetah," Steve said, finally regaining his strength. "Better to give up now. Trust me on this."

The other officers were beginning to move. Cheetah had to think fast. She noticed a panel in the ceiling.

That must be an air duct, she thought. *I can use it to escape this place.*

Cheetah leaped into the air, tore the panel off with her claws, and crawled inside. She scurried through the building's ventilation shaft, looking for a way out.

"We've got to find Cheetah. *Now,*" Steve said, rising to his feet. "If she finds her way to the Black Room, we're all in trouble. I'm calling in a specialist to handle this one."

As Steve radioed for help, Cheetah slithered through the air ducts as fast as she could. Finding the exit was difficult since she had no idea where she was going. A.R.G.U.S. headquarters was filled with many secret chambers and any one of them could lead to the outside world.

After crawling for a while, Cheetah noticed the ceiling panels below her felt warm. A draft of air moved through the duct.

This must mean I'm close to freedom, Cheetah thought. She followed the trail of warm ceiling panels to a vent at a dead end. *Here goes nothing!*

Cheetah tore off the vent and plunged through ceiling. She found herself in the middle of the mysterious Black Room. It wasn't exactly where she'd planned to go, but it was a new chance to cause trouble.

Cheetah had heard rumors about the Black Room for many years. Her villainous friends said it was the place A.R.G.U.S. stored the world's most dangerous items after they'd been taken from their owners.

The villain looked around. The room held magic spears, mystical helmets, and contraptions of all kinds. She soon came upon an ancient drawing.

"What do we have here?" Cheetah said in a playful tone. She wiped the dust away and discovered it was a map to the fabled Pandora's Box.

Ancient myths say Pandora's Box contains great power, Cheetah thought as she studied the map carefully. *Maybe I can use that power to become human again? I could change back to the person I was before my experiments turned me into an animal.*

Cheetah pondered her future until a loud crash snapped her out of her daydream.

CA·THOOM!

The door to the Black Room burst open. Wonder Woman had arrived!

"Put that scroll down, Cheetah," the super hero warned. "I know you're capable of ending this peacefully."

"You know nothing!" Cheetah growled. She bit down on the scroll and attacked Wonder Woman, swiping her deadly claws in every direction.

The Amazon warrior used her silver bracelets to block the attack. Cheetah threw a kick, but Wonder Woman caught it in midair. She tossed Cheetah away and into a nearby wall. The blow wasn't enough to stop the super-villain.

"Is that all you've got?" Cheetah asked, circling her prey. "Why don't you show me what you're really made of?"

Wonder Woman eyed Cheetah cautiously. The villain's animal side could be savage and uncontrollable. The hero hoped her human side was still in there somewhere and willing to listen.

"I don't want to fight you," Wonder Woman said. "But I will if it means saving your life."

"Shut it, Amazon!" Cheetah smirked. "I can't bear to hear another one of your sappy pep talks."

"Very well then. I'll cut straight to the point," Wonder Woman said. "You're out of options. Surrender now, Barbara Ann. We both know it's the only choice."

"Don't you dare call me by that name!" Cheetah exclaimed. She clutched the map in her hands. "When I find Pandora's Box, I'll return to my human form once again."

Wonder Woman made her way toward her enemy. "That's not how Pandora's Box works," she said. "You need to trust me."

Cheetah became angrier. "You want *me* to trust *you?*" she snarled. "Not a chance!"

Wonder Woman grabbed her magic lasso and flung it toward Cheetah. The villain caught the rope before it could entangle her. Cheetah yanked it, sending Wonder Woman flying across the room and crashing into a pile of empty metal crates.

"You don't understand!" Cheetah exclaimed. "I've been cursed. My thoughts are dark and clouded. I want to be myself again! Don't you get it?!"

Wonder Woman pushed the crates off her body. "This is not the way. You've got to fight your animal instincts," she said. "I want to help you. Surrender and we'll find a way to change you back together."

"Empty promises," Cheetah scoffed. "I've heard them all before." She picked up a large barrel and threw it at Wonder Woman.

The Amazon Princess swiftly ducked for cover. The barrel smashed into the wall, covering the area with strange liquid. Three small, worm-like creatures wiggled out of the wreckage.

At first, Wonder Woman didn't think anything of them. As small as they were, they didn't appear to be an immediate threat. What she didn't know was that the liquid they'd been kept in prevented the worms from growing.

Now exposed to the air, the worms grew into enormous beasts. Their once soft exteriors hardened into protective armor. Sharp pincers burst from their bodies as their red eyes bulged. In a matter of seconds, the worms became frightening, nightmarish creatures. They headed straight for Wonder Woman.

"Merciful Minerva!" Wonder Woman gasped. She lassoed one of the beasts, but it whipped her around the room wildly.

While Wonder Woman was busy, Cheetah strolled through the Black Room looking for something new to use on her enemy. A glowing red jewel caught her eye.

"What do *you* do?" she said, gazing at the gem.

CHAPTER 2

NIGHTMARE

"Yield, beasts!" Wonder Woman shouted. She rode the back of one worm creature while trying to lasso another. It was no easy task. A third worm creature lunged for Cheetah, but Wonder Woman jumped in to save her. She leaped onto the beast's neck and used all her might to steer it away from her enemy.

These monsters are uncontrollable, Wonder Woman thought. *I'll have to use my wits if I'm going to defeat them.*

Wonder Woman hopped off the creature and raced to the corner of the Black Room. She positioned herself for battle.

"Come and get me!" she exclaimed.

Wonder Woman grabbed her lasso and swung it through the air. The rope's golden glow captivated the worm creatures as they slithered forward. Once they got close, Wonder Woman used her super-speed to run circles around the worms, creating a cocoon with her lasso that encased them completely.

"*That* should hold you," she said.

"Those beasts should be the least of your worries," Cheetah said, clutching the red gem tightly.

"Put that gem down before you do something you regret," Wonder Woman said. "This is your last chance, Cheetah."

"You're right about that, Wonder Woman. This *is* my last chance," Cheetah said. "To free myself of this curse!"

Cheetah held the glowing jewel in the air, bathing her body in its bright red light. In an instant, she returned to her human form.

"I've done it. I'm *me* again!" Cheetah exclaimed. Then she heard the sound of approaching A.R.G.U.S. officers in the distance.

The villain aimed the gem toward the door and concentrated with all her mental might. A blast of red energy shot from inside the gem. It sealed the door to the Black Room so no one else could enter.

"No interruptions," Cheetah said.

Wonder Woman wasn't sure what was happening, but she knew it wasn't good.

The hero took off like a bolt and grabbed hold of the gem, but Cheetah wouldn't let go. She held the powerful jewel tightly, yanking it back from Wonder Woman's grasp. The two rivals struggled for control of the gem, neither one willing to give an inch.

"Hands off!" Cheetah warned. She and Wonder Woman squeezed the gem at the exact same moment and a burst of red light filled the entire room.

When the glow faded, they realized they'd been transported to a beautiful island paradise. The air was crisp and clean, and the sun shone bright in the cloudless sky. The island was filled with ancient temples and a lush forest, surrounded by a clear blue ocean on all sides. They were on the island of Themyscira, Wonder Woman's childhood home and birthplace of the Amazons.

Cheetah noticed her enemy's shock and jerked the gem from her grasp so Wonder Woman couldn't grab it.

"What is this place?" Cheetah said.

"I'm home!" Wonder Woman gasped. "I'm not sure what's happening but . . ."

"Diana?" a voice called out from nearby. Wonder Woman looked in all directions, but she couldn't find where it had come from.

"What are you doing here?" the voice called out once more. Wonder Woman turned to find Queen Hippolyta standing behind her.

"Mother!" Wonder Woman exclaimed. She extended her arms to give the queen a hug but was pushed away.

"I asked you a question, Diana. What are you doing here?" Hippolyta demanded. "I told you never to come back!"

Wonder Woman was confused by the queen's strange behavior. "But Mother that's not true," she said. "I've *always* been welcome here. This is my home."

Queen Hippolyta's tone darkened. "You've *failed* me, Diana. You've *failed* your sisters. You were to bring peace to the outside world, yet it boils with war," she exclaimed. "You are a shame to the Amazons."

Wonder Woman couldn't believe what she was hearing. Amazon warriors sprang forth from the surrounding woods wearing battle armor and carrying weapons. They didn't look pleased.

Wonder Woman spotted two familiar faces in the crowd. "Philipus? Aunt Antiope? I don't understand what's happening," she said. "If I have wronged you all in some way, please forgive me."

"No more lies!" Hippolyta shouted. "Amazons attack!"

As the Amazons raised their weapons, they released a fearsome cheer. Wonder Woman was no longer their sister; she was their enemy.

"I see you're without your lasso. What a terrible shame," sneered Antiope. She grabbed her bow and fired off a series of arrows in Wonder Woman's direction.

Diana crossed arms and deflected the assault with her enchanted silver bracelets. "Don't do this," she pleaded. "We're family, Antiope. Fight whatever is controlling you!"

This is going to be good, Cheetah thought. She hid behind a temple to watch the battle from a safe distance, clinging to the red gem with all her might.

Philipus sneaked up behind Wonder Woman and surprised her.

"Nothing is controlling us, Princess," Philipus said. "We've finally seen the light."

Philipus grabbed Wonder Woman's neck, but Diana was ready. She flipped the Amazon warrior over her shoulder and onto the ground.

"I do not wish to fight you," Wonder Woman said. "Stand down. Please!"

BOOM! BOOM! BOOM!

A loud pounding echoed throughout the island. It was as if someone was trapped in a metal box, trying to escape. A faint male voice called out, "It's not real, Diana. It's just a dream!"

The voice startled Wonder Woman. *It sounds so familiar,* she thought.

"Fraud!" Philipus shouted, kicking Wonder Woman to the ground and putting her in another headlock. The hero struggled to break free.

BOOM! BOOM! BOOM!

The strange pounding returned. This time the sound shook the ground like an earthquake.

"Cheetah is using the Dreamstone to trick you," the mystery voice revealed. "You've got to fight for control!"

Wonder Woman finally recognized the voice. "Steve!" she exclaimed. "Now I know what I must do."

When Diana was a little girl, she'd often get frustrated with her studies. Whenever that happened, Queen Hippolyta told her to simply close her eyes, take a deep breath, and focus on something positive.

"This will make the dark clouds part so that you can see the sunshine once again," Hippolyta would say. It was a valuable piece of advice that Diana had always kept close.

Wonder Woman relaxed and closed her eyes. She took a deep breath and focused on ending her nightmare.

"I will not believe these lies any longer!" she shouted.

In a sudden flash of red, the Amazons vanished into thin air.

"No," Hippolyta whispered. Then another flash of red filled the sky and the queen disappeared as well.

Wonder Woman opened her eyes. She was relieved to find herself safe at last.

I may be safe from one threat, but the struggle isn't over yet, she thought.

"You always ruin everything!" Cheetah exclaimed. The villain came out from her hiding place, still in her human form. She trembled as she held the glowing red stone.

"This isn't real, Cheetah," Wonder Woman said, her tone calm and kind. She could see the pain in her enemy's eyes. "That gem makes you see what you want to see, but it's a lie. Allow me to help you."

"I won't let you change me back!" Cheetah squeezed the gem once more.

FWASH! In a final burst of red light, Themyscira disappeared and Wonder Woman lost consciousness inside the Black Room.

THOOM! The door blasted open as Steve Trevor and a fleet of A.R.G.U.S. officers flooded in to secure the area. Steve rushed to check on Wonder Woman, who was just waking up.

"You okay?" Steve asked.

"I think so," Wonder Woman replied. "How long have I been in here?"

"Not too long," Steve replied. "Maybe two or three minutes tops."

Wonder Woman couldn't believe her ears. "It felt like an eternity. What was that red gem Cheetah used? I've never experienced anything like it," she said.

"That was the Dreamstone. A.R.G.U.S. swiped it from a bad guy called Dr. Destiny," Steve explained. "We locked it up in here so it couldn't do any harm. Whoever holds the Dreamstone can change the world around them however they want. It may *seem* real, but it's all just a trick of the mind."

"I see," Wonder Woman said. "Now I know why we ended up on Themyscira."

"Why's that?" asked Steve.

"The Dreamstone must have combined my thoughts with Cheetah's when we were wrestling for control of it," said Wonder Woman. "Thank you for helping me see the light. But where's Cheetah?"

"She escaped through the air ducts. I got a report on my radio that she took off in an A.R.G.U.S. jump ship," said Steve.

"I must find her right away," Wonder Woman said.

Steve handed Wonder Woman her magic lasso. "That's not all, I'm afraid," he said.

"What do you mean?" the Amazon asked.

"The good news is that Cheetah dropped the Dreamstone on her way out," Steve replied. "The bad news is she took the map to Pandora's Box."

CHAPTER 3

OPERATION: FIND CHEETAH

"I must leave at once," Wonder Woman said. "If Cheetah finds Pandora's Box, she'll have the power to destroy the planet. It won't be a dream, it'll be a nightmare—and a real one at that. I have to find her and stop her."

"That's not going to be as easy as it looks. Thankfully, we've got someone here at A.R.G.U.S. who can help," said Steve.

Wonder Woman didn't want help. She was anxious to begin the search by herself.

"Cheetah is *my* responsibility. I will handle this mission alone," she said. "I can't risk more innocent people getting hurt."

Steve greatly admired Wonder Woman's commitment to justice. He could see the pressures of being a hero causing her stress. As her good friend, he offered up a few words of encouragement.

"You just wrestled three giant worms and fought your way through a crazy dream world," Steve said. "Not to mention that you stopped Cheetah from unleashing all the other bad stuff in the Black Room. We're grateful you showed up when you did. You saved a lot of lives. Don't be so hard on yourself."

"Thanks for the reminder, Steve," Wonder Woman said. "I must take a moment to clear my head."

Wonder Woman looked around the room. "You mentioned there was someone here at A.R.G.U.S. who can help us track Cheetah," she said. "Where is this person now?"

Steve smiled and pointed behind Wonder Woman. She turned to find A.R.G.U.S. Agent Etta Candy headed her way. They were good friends who'd worked together many times in the past.

"It's great to see you, Diana," Etta said. "Even under such horrible conditions."

"I feel at ease knowing you're on the case," said Wonder Woman. "What can you tell us, Etta?"

Etta used her touchpad to activate a glowing green hologram of the Greek island of Santorini. Steve and Wonder Woman carefully studied its features.

"While we know Pandora's Box is located somewhere on the island, its exact whereabouts are a mystery without the map," Etta explained.

"Well that's just great," Steve said. "Got any good news?"

"As a matter of fact, I do," Etta said. She pressed a button on her touchpad and a blinking blue light appeared on the holographic map.

"Years ago I put a microscopic tracking chip on the back of the map just in case something ever happened to it," Etta explained. "The blue light shows us where the map is located at any given moment."

"Wherever the map is located, that's where Cheetah will be," said Wonder Woman. "Brilliant!"

Etta traced her finger along the hologram, following the blue light's path. "She's definitely headed to Santorini," she said.

"Great! Wonder Woman can go grab her, bring her back, and we can all go out for ice cream after," Steve said.

"It won't be that easy. Santorini is a busy vacation spot. There are tourists everywhere," Etta explained.

"Which means innocent lives may be in danger," said Wonder Woman. "I'll have to be doubly careful."

"I've got some more news. Cheetah's stolen jump ship comes with a holographic disguise kit. She'll be able to change her look in order to blend into the crowd," Etta said. "Finding her won't be as easy as it seems, even with that tracking device."

Wonder Woman took a moment to consider the situation. "I'll proceed with caution," she said. "Thank you, Etta. Your insights are always valuable."

"No problem, Diana. Always happy to help," Etta said. She handed her a small device. "You'll need this to track the map. I hope Cheetah learns her lesson."

As Wonder Woman prepared to leave A.R.G.U.S. headquarters, Steve chased after her. "Are you sure you want to do this?" he asked.

Wonder Woman smiled. "I've battled mad gods from other realms. I've stopped alien invasions. I'm a member of the Justice League," she said. "There is no one more suited to this mission than I am."

"Cheetah really wants to hurt you," said Steve. "She won't be stopped so easily."

"Lives are in danger, Steve. I was sent here to protect them. I'm prepared to face whatever dangers await," said Wonder Woman.

"Very well," Steve replied, handing Wonder Woman a small pouch. "But take this with you, just in case."

"What's this?" asked Wonder Woman.

"You'll see," said Steve. "Think of it as an insurance policy. If things get too crazy, you might want to use what's inside to help straighten Cheetah out. Just make sure it doesn't fall into the wrong hands," he said. "Oh, and don't forget these electronic cuffs to bring her back in."

"Thank you," said Wonder Woman. She dropped the cuffs into the pouch and hooked it to her belt. "See you when I return."

Wonder Woman exited A.R.G.U.S. headquarters and boarded her Invisible Jet, which she'd parked in a hangar above the secret facility. She soon took off into the sky.

* * *

Wonder Woman quietly landed the jet on the outskirts of Santorini, making sure not to draw attention to herself. As she made her way toward the city square, it became obvious this mission was going to be harder than she thought.

A festive carnival was taking place. Music blared loudly as partygoers danced in the streets. There were people in costumes, tossing beaded necklaces at one another. Everyone was having fun and enjoying themselves without a care in the world. They had no clue Cheetah was lurking among them.

BEEP! BEEP! BEEP!

The device Etta gave Wonder Woman showed that the map was nearby. But with so many people in one place, it was difficult to pinpoint Cheetah's exact location.

This isn't going to be easy, Wonder Woman thought. *There's too much commotion. I have to keep a low profile, or Cheetah might see me coming and do something dangerous. I'll need to be extra careful.*

Diana covered herself with a cloak and moved through the crowd in silence, keeping her eyes peeled for trouble. *Any one of these partygoers could be Cheetah in disguise,* she thought.

Wonder Woman spotted an angry man storming through the crowd, pushing people aside. His behavior was suspicious.

"You!" Wonder Woman said, pointing at the woman. "Don't move!"

It was Cheetah in disguise! "I guess I don't need this anymore," the villain said, turning off the holographic disguise. In an instant her full-body mask disappeared to reveal her animal form.

"Run for your lives!" a man cried out. The once-happy citizens grew frightened. They ran screaming in all directions, hoping to escape. But the crowd was too thick. No one could move.

Cheetah leaped onto an awning to avoid the chaos she'd created. She watched with delight as people trampled one another to get away.

It's time to cause even more trouble, Cheetah thought. *These old structures aren't as solid as they used to be. I can use that to my advantage.*

The villain leaped from one awning to the next, climbing higher and higher until she reached the top of one of Santorini's oldest buildings. There she found a bell tower made of four stone slabs. After many years of wear and tear, it looked as if it could break apart at any minute.

"Watch out below!" Cheetah exclaimed. She used her strength to topple the bell tower, causing it to fall toward the crowd.

Wonder Woman jumped into action. She tossed away her cloak, flew in like a bolt, and caught the stone tower before it crushed a group of tourists. After gently placing it on the ground, Wonder Woman turned her attention to her enemy.

"Leave these people alone, Cheetah," Wonder Woman said. "It's me you want. No one else has to get hurt."

"What I want is Pandora's Box. This is your last warning—*stay out of my way!*" exclaimed Cheetah. She hopped down from her perch and took off on foot. She zigzagged through the streets of Santorini, disappearing into the crowd.

"There!" a woman shouted. She pointed Wonder Woman toward a series of ancient caves on the mountainside nearby. Cheetah was headed straight for them. "Be careful, Wonder Woman. Those caves hide many dangers," the woman said. "Remain cautious."

"Thank you," said Wonder Woman. Then she took off to stop Cheetah once and for all.

CHAPTER 4

DANGER LURKS

As Wonder Woman climbed up the jagged mountainside, she wondered what threats she'd face in the caves. Pandora's Box had been hidden by ancient, magical forces whose aim was to keep the cursed item safe from meddlers.

I must pay extra careful attention to my surroundings, Wonder Woman thought. *There will no doubt be traps laid to prevent trespassers from retrieving the box.*

Upon reaching the mountaintop, Wonder Woman faced a choice. Three caves stood before her. She didn't know which one to choose.

"*This* way, Wonder Woman," a soft voice whispered from inside the left cave.

"No, *this* way, Wonder Woman," a deep voice called out from inside the right cave.

Wonder Woman wasn't about to fall for any tricks. She studied the ground and noticed Cheetah's footsteps leading into the middle cave. She followed them with caution.

Entering the darkened cavern, Wonder Woman spotted a series of ancient drawings on the wall—a black sun, furious storms, and fire covering a mountain. They were dark omens meant to scare people away from searching for Pandora's Box.

Wonder Woman, however, didn't hesitate. She took one of the torches that lined the cave walls and used it to light her path. As she walked through the tunnel, she came upon an open area littered with skeletons.

These bones have been here a very long time, she thought. *Many explorers have come here looking for treasure, but few have escaped with their lives. I must be on the right path.*

Wonder Woman took a step and felt the ground shift ever so slightly.

THWIP! THWIP! THWIP! THWIP!

Small wooden spikes shot from all sides. Wonder Woman raised her bracelets at the speed of light, deflecting each and every one.

That was close, she thought. *But there are more dangers to face. I need to be extra sure that's the last of those spikes. It's time for a test.*

Wonder Woman found two heavy rocks and rolled one of them across the tunnel floor. This time, a new series of wooden spikes rained down from the cavern ceiling and clattered onto the floor.

I knew it, the hero thought. *Let's see if there are any more.*

Wonder Woman rolled the second rock through the tunnel. This time nothing happened. No new attacks were triggered. The Amazon warrior breathed a sigh of relief and continued on her way.

Wonder Woman soon faced yet another choice. The cavern forked in two directions. It was time to use the tracking device Etta had given her.

Wonder Woman turned the device on. To her surprise, nothing happened. Suddenly, high-pitched chirping filled the tunnel.

I'd know that sound anywhere, she thought.

A large colony of bats stormed through one of the caverns, swarming the area. They disoriented Wonder Woman, blinding her and throwing her off balance. The hero dropped to the ground.

Seconds later the bats were gone, but Wonder Woman was shaken. The tracking device no longer worked, and she wasn't sure which path was correct. She decided to let her intuition guide her.

The dark forces at work to stop me are clever. They assume those bats will warn me away from the direction they came, she thought, *but that's exactly where I'll go.*

As Wonder Woman made her way into the bat cave, the space became narrower. Then a dull roar echoed throughout the entire cavern.

RUMBLE! RUMBLE! RUMBLE!

The ground under Wonder Woman's feet vibrated. She wondered if it was an earthquake until she spotted the source of the shaking. A giant boulder was headed in her direction. It had been spit out like a pinball from deep within the cave. Inside the cramped space, Wonder Woman had nowhere to go but back.

I don't want to turn back, but I may not have a choice, the hero thought.

Before Wonder Woman could move, a rock wall crashed down behind her.

KA-THOOM!

She was trapped with nowhere to run.

There's no stopping that speeding boulder, Wonder Woman thought. *I've been left with only one option. I must stand my ground.*

Wonder Woman braced herself and made a tight fist. When the boulder arrived, she punched it with all her might.

BOOM!

The giant rock shattered into a million pieces, covering her in a pile of gravel. Using her super-strength, Wonder Woman dug herself out of the rubble, tossing boulder fragments away from her body with ease.

Once free, Wonder Woman dusted herself off and continued along the path. Nothing was going to stop her now. She soon came to the end of the tunnel where Cheetah stood waiting.

"What took you so long?" Cheetah sneered.

"How did *you* make it this far into the cave?" Wonder Woman asked.

Cheetah grinned. "Don't you know? Cats have nine lives," she said. "And I'll have even more lives once I open this."

Cheetah held up a small cube made of tarnished metal. She'd found Pandora's Box! She hugged it tightly, rubbing it like a good luck charm.

"Don't come any closer, Amazon!" the villain barked.

Wonder Woman wanted to run and grab the box, but the move was too risky. Cheetah was just as fast as her and could open the box before she got her hands on it.

The hero decided to be patient for the moment. The situation required a different approach.

"How did you make it through the cave's many dangers?" Wonder Woman asked.

"I faced no dangers. The dark forces protecting Pandora's Box must recognize me as a kindred spirit. It seems we share the same evil intentions," Cheetah said.

"Once you open that box, everything will change," Wonder Woman said.

"That's what I'm hoping for," purred Cheetah.

"So why wait? Open it and see what happens," Wonder Woman taunted.

Cheetah sensed a trap. "Don't test me!" she exclaimed. "I'm not playing games."

"We both know why you're hesitating, Cheetah. It's because deep down you know Pandora's Box will only bring more pain and misery," said Wonder Woman. "Barbara Ann Minerva was a brilliant scientist. I know she's still inside you."

"Stop saying that name," Cheetah growled.

"Use your head. You've made some mistakes, but you can always turn things around," Wonder Woman said. "Make the right choice. Begin a new path."

A somber look fell upon Cheetah's face. "I've made too many mistakes," she said. "There's no turning back now."

"I was afraid you'd say that," Wonder Woman replied. She reached into the pouch Steve had given her and revealed its contents.

"The Dreamstone," Cheetah whispered. "What are you doing?!"

Wonder Woman squeezed the glowing red gem, transporting them both to a peaceful green field. The sun was bright and the cheerful sounds of wildlife filled the air.

"What is this?" Cheetah asked.

"When we struggled over the Dreamstone in the Black Room, it combined my dreams with yours," Wonder Woman explained. "But this time the dream is all mine."

Cheetah looked down to find her body had become human again. "Now you mock me by giving me what I want," she sneered. "Why are you doing this?"

"Don't you see? We want the same things. Take a deep breath. Clear your mind. Don't let your animal instincts control you," Wonder Woman said. "There's always a peaceful solution. It may not be easy to achieve, but it's possible."

Wonder Woman strolled through the lush field, motioning for Cheetah to join. "Walk with me?" asked Wonder Woman. "Please."

Cheetah hesitated. "Why?" she asked.

"Listen carefully, Cheetah. Pandora's Box is filled with an ancient and unpredictable evil," Wonder Woman said. "You won't find what you seek by opening it. Give it to me so that I may dispose of it properly. Then you and I will find a way to change you back into the woman you once were. You have my word."

"But what about my crimes?" Cheetah asked. "I'll be locked away forever."

Wonder Woman struggled to find the right thing to say. She feared the wrong words might cause Cheetah to make a bad decision.

"You'll need to pay for your mistakes, yes. But that doesn't mean you can't use your brilliant mind to help others," Wonder Woman said. "Please. Stop this insanity."

Cheetah smiled as she held Pandora's Box. "Thank you for showing me who I really am, Wonder Woman," Cheetah said. She grabbed the Dreamstone and crushed it with her bare hands. In an instant, the peaceful dreamscape melted away, returning them to the dark reality inside the cave.

"What are you doing?" Wonder Woman gasped.

"Something I should have done a long time ago," Cheetah replied with a sneer. She opened Pandora's Box. "Say goodbye, Wonder Woman!"

CHAPTER 5

CHAOS ERUPTS

KABOOM!

The mountain shook as lightning crashed inside the cavern. Cheetah's body pulsed with evil power. Pandora's Box had been opened and a great darkness prepared to consume the planet.

"Cheetah, what have you done?" Wonder Woman asked.

Cheetah's hollow eyes glowed bright. Her fingers crackled with energy. "I've never felt such power before," she said. "And, to think, you tried to take it all away from me."

Evil phantoms emerged from inside the box. They swirled through the air toward Wonder Woman, rocketing past her and out into the world.

"These forces you've unleashed will destroy everything in their path. I'm begging you to close the box," pleaded Wonder Woman.

"Never," the villain sneered. With a twist of her wrist, Cheetah sent a bolt of blazing lightning in Wonder Woman's direction. It blasted the ground beneath her feet, sending her flying through the air.

Wonder Woman shook off the attack and formed a plan. *The people need me,* she thought. *I must go help them.*

"Think about what you're doing, Cheetah," Wonder Woman said. "It doesn't have to be this way. Remember that."

Wonder Woman flew through the cave at top speed, blasting through the layers of rock that had fallen on the path. When she finally reached the entrance, she was shocked by the sight stretching out before her.

The sky had turned black and red. Lightning bolts blazed through the clouds. Fires had broken out all over the island. The phantoms that had been trapped within the box now swirled over the countryside. Scared citizens scattered to escape the chaos.

I don't even know where to begin, Wonder Woman thought. *This is madness.*

"Help!" a man cried out. "Help us!"

Wonder Woman spotted a little girl and her parents on the cliffs below her. Their car had broken down, and they were trapped by raging fires. The hero quickly flew down to help them.

"Grab on to me as tightly as you can," she said. "Everything will be all right."

Wonder Woman scooped up the little girl, who hugged her extra close. Her parents huddled around the Amazon Princess and together they flew out of harm's way. Wonder Woman took them to a clear area at the base of the mountain far away from the danger.

As Wonder Woman turned to leave the family, a powerful earthquake rocked the island.

RUMBLE! RUMBLE! RUMBLE!

The ground jolted back and forth. Giant sinkholes opened up across the island, swallowing trees, buildings, and anything else above them. Worst of all, the vibrations awakened a sleeping volcano. Rivers of molten lava spewed from the top of the volcano, oozing toward the town below.

I've got to act fast or that lava will burn everything to a crisp! Wonder Woman thought.

The Amazon began tossing boulders, one after the other, to build a wall between the town and the flowing lava. But it wasn't enough. The lava piled up and threatened to flow right over the top of the wall.

Wonder Woman devised a new plan. She dug her fingers into the mountainside and ripped off a huge, curved rock slab. She used it to scoop out a pathway that led straight to the ocean. The new channel allowed the lava to flow around the town completely.

As the lava hissed and steamed into the water, Wonder Woman realized her work was far from over. She looked up to find Cheetah standing at the top of the volcano, her hands wrapped around Pandora's Box. Wonder Woman zoomed up to face her.

"How's it going, Wonder Woman? Tired yet?" Cheetah asked.

"Not a bit," Wonder Woman replied. "Do your worst. I'll be here to stop you."

"Ugh. You think you're so good," Cheetah screeched. "Little miss perfect hero, always doing the right thing. I'm sick of it."

"I'm not perfect by a long shot. I try my best. That's all," Wonder Woman said. "Look around you, Cheetah. Do you see the destruction you've caused? Only you can end this. Close the box."

"I've caused you a lot of trouble, haven't I? I suppose that makes me happy," Cheetah said. "But I still haven't gotten what I want."

"And you never will!" Wonder Woman exclaimed. "Pandora's Box doesn't grant wishes. It just causes pain and suffering."

"For you!" Cheetah exclaimed.

A wave of phantoms swarmed Wonder Woman, stealing her energy and weakening her body. She fell to her knees.

"Help me, Cheetah," Wonder Woman cried. "You're not an animal, you're a human being. If there's a shred of goodness inside you, you'll stop these attacks and return things to normal."

Cheetah looked across the island. Her actions had brought massive destruction to everything around her. Fires raged. The earth had torn itself apart. And yet she was unchanged. She was still trapped inside her animal form. Pandora's Box had failed her. Cheetah realized that Wonder Woman had been right all along.

RUMBLE! RUMBLE! RUMBLE!

Another earthquake, this one stronger than ever, rocked the mountainside. Cheetah lost her footing and fell into the volcano.

"No!" Wonder Woman shouted.

Though she was too weak to fly, Wonder Woman crawled to the side of the volcano. Below her, just out of reach, Cheetah stood on a small ledge. She was safe for the moment but not out of harm's way just yet. The lava below bubbled and splashed closer and closer. Soon it would reach the ledge.

Wonder Woman tossed one end of her magic lasso down to Cheetah. "Take hold of this!" she exclaimed.

Cheetah wrapped the lasso tightly around one hand as she grasped Pandora's Box with the other. Then Wonder Woman yanked and pulled the villain up. Cheetah could feel the lava almost nipping at her feet.

"Pull, Amazon, pull!" she screeched. Inch by inch Cheetah rose, until she could safely crawl over the lip of the volcano.

Out of breath, the two exhausted enemies stood atop the volcano. Cheetah held the open box high in the sky.

"Return everything to the way it was!" she shouted.

In a flash of lightning and thunder, the box swiftly sucked the phantoms back inside. The earth stopped shaking. The volcano cooled. The nightmare was over at last.

Wonder Woman closed the lid, locked it, and took the box from Cheetah.

"Thank you," the hero said. Then she gave Cheetah a hug.

"Why did you hug me?" Cheetah asked. "I tried to destroy you."

"We've all suffered enough for today," Wonder Woman said. "You've been through a great ordeal, Barbara Ann. Do you now understand that violence isn't the answer?"

Cheetah looked Wonder Woman square in the eye. "I think I do but my mind is so clouded. All I know is that I don't want to fight you anymore. I just want things to go back to the way they were," she said. "I promise I'll try to be better. Will you still help me?"

"Of course," Wonder Woman replied. Then she removed the pair of electronic cuffs from her pouch and snapped them onto Cheetah's wrists.

"What happened? What came over me?" Cheetah asked. "Why did I just say all of that? Did you do some kind of Amazon voodoo on me?!"

"Not at all. Everything you said came from your heart. You were tangled in my magic lasso," Wonder Woman said, unwrapping the lasso from Cheetah's wrist. "It made you tell the truth."

Cheetah looked annoyed. She hadn't planned on being so honest.

"Ugh!" she groaned. "Just toss me in your stupid jet and take me back to prison."

And Wonder Woman did just that.

CHEETAH

REAL NAME:
Barbara Ann Minerva

SPECIES:
Mutated Human

OCCUPATION:
Biologist

HEIGHT:
5 feet 9 inches

WEIGHT:
120 pounds

EYES:
Green

HAIR:
Auburn

POWERS/ABILITIES:
Superhuman strength, speed, and agility. Her claws and teeth are razor sharp, capable of slicing through stone.

BIOGRAPHY:

Cheetah was once an accomplished scientist named Barbara Ann Minerva. She was tireless in her effort to enhance humans with animal abilities. When funding for her project was cut off, Minerva chose to experiment on herself. The results were terrifying. She'd become a hybrid creature that was half-human, half-cheetah. Though she now possessed increased strength and the enhanced abilities of the cheetah, her mind was fractured. She'd developed a villainous streak that led her to commit crimes. Though she's fallen in with a variety of criminal organizations, deep within Cheetah there's still a part of her that hopes to one day become normal again.

· Cheetah doesn't always work alone. She once joined forces with Lex Luthor as a member of his Injustice Gang. The villainess has also worked with Gorilla Grodd in his Legion of Doom.

· Cheetah is Wonder Woman's most cunning and clever enemy. Her catlike agility and super-strength make her a formidable fighter too. To make matters worse, Cheetah is prone to animal-like rages at any given moment.

· Cheetah can put up a good fight, but she's no match for Wonder Woman's Lasso of Truth. The golden rope can ensnare the villainess, weakening her super-speed and super-strength. More importantly, the lasso always gets to the root of Cheetah's trickery by forcing her to speak nothing but the truth.

BIOGRAPHIES

Brandon T. Snider has authored more than 75 books featuring pop culture icons such as Captain Picard, Transformers, and the Muppets. Additionally, he's written books for Cartoon Network favorites such as *Adventure Time*, *Regular Show*, and *Powerpuff Girls*. He's best known for the top-selling *DC Comics Ultimate Character Guide* and the award-winning *Dark Knight Manual*. Brandon lives in New York City and is a member of the Writer's Guild of America.

Luciano Vecchio was born in 1982 and is based in Buenos Aires, Argentina. As a freelance artist for many projects at Marvel and DC Comics, his work has been seen in print and online around the world. He has illustrated many DC Super Heroes books for Capstone, and some of his recent comic work includes *Beware the Batman*, *Green Lantern: The Animated Series*, *Young Justice*, *Ultimate Spider-Man*, and his creator owned web-comic, *Sereno*.

GLOSSARY

hologram (HOL-uh-gram)—an image made by laser beams that looks three-dimensional

instinct (IN-stingkt)—behavior that is natural rather than learned

intuition (in-too-ISH-uhn)—a feeling about something that can't be explained logically

omen (OH-muhn)—a sign of something that will happen in the future

phantom (FAN-tuhm)—a ghost

sinkhole (SINGK-hohl)—a hollow place in the ground

suspicious (suh-SPISH-uhs)—seeming distrustful

terrace (TER-iss)—an open porch or a paved area just outside a house

transport (transs-PORT)—to move or carry something or someone from one place to another

trespasser (TRESS-pass-uhr)—someone who enters someone else's property without permission

ventilation shaft (ven-tuh-LAY-shuhn SHAFT)—a narrow passage or duct that carries fresh air throughout a building

voodoo (VOO-doo)—a magic that can control someone's actions

DISCUSSION QUESTIONS

1. Even though they're enemies, Wonder Woman tries to help Cheetah. Have you ever helped someone you didn't get along with? Did things work out the way you thought they would? Explain.

2. Wonder Woman had to escape several deadly traps to pass through the caves, but Cheetah did not. Why do you think Cheetah was able to find Pandora's Box so easily?

3. At the end of the story, Wonder Woman saves Cheetah from the lava and even gives the villain a hug. Did her actions surprise you? Discuss why they did or did not.

WRITING PROMPTS

1. Cheetah opens Pandora's Box even though Wonder Woman tells her bad things will happen if she does. Write about a time when you did something even though a friend warned you not to. Describe what happened.

2. If you had a Dreamstone, what kind of world would you create with it? What would it look like? How would people behave? Write a paragraph describing your world in detail.

3. Cheetah uses her catlike animal powers to battle Wonder Woman. If you could have the powers of any animal, which would you choose? Write a short paragraph describing your powers and draw a picture of what you would look like.